*This book belongs to*

...........................................................................................

# Walt Disney's Peter Pan

Disney
Storybook Favourites
Reader's Digest Young Families

SKULL ROCK

# Walt Disney's
# Peter Pan

Illustrations by The Walt Disney Studios

Story adapted by Monique Peterson

Illustrations adapted by
John Hench and Al Dempster

CROCODILE CREEK

MERMAID LAGOON

On a quiet street in London lived the Darling family. There was Father and Mother Darling, and Wendy, Michael and John. There was also the children's nursemaid, Nana – a Saint Bernard dog.

For Nana and the children, the best hour of the day was bedtime, for then they were all together in the nursery. There Wendy told wonderful stories about Peter Pan of Never Land. This Never Land was a magical spot with Indians and mermaids and fairies – and wicked pirates, too.

John and Michael liked best of all to play pirates. They had some fine, slashing duels between Peter Pan and his arch-enemy, the pirate, Captain Hook.

Father Darling did not like this kind of rough play. He blamed it on Wendy's stories of Peter Pan, and Father Darling did not approve of those stories, either.

'It is time for Wendy to grow up,' he said. 'This is your last night in the nursery, Wendy.'

All the children were very upset at that news. Without Wendy in the nursery there would be no more Peter Pan stories! Then, to make matters worse, Father Darling decided there would be no more dog nursemaids. The children were very sad indeed. So he tied Nana in the garden for the night.

When Mother and Father Darling had gone out for the evening, leaving the children snug in their beds with Nana on guard below, who should come to the nursery but Peter Pan! Peter told them that he had been secretly flying in from Never Land all along to listen, unseen, to the bedtime stories.

But the night before, Nana had caught sight of Peter and nipped off his shadow as he had escaped. So back he had come, looking for his lost shadow and hoping to hear a story about himself.

With him was a fairy, named Tinker Bell. When Peter heard that Wendy was to be sent from the nursery, he hit upon a plan.

'I'll take you to Never Land with me, to tell stories to my Lost Boys!' he exclaimed as Wendy sewed his shadow back on.

Wendy thought that was a lovely idea – but only if Michael and John could go, too. So Peter Pan taught them all to fly – with happy thoughts and faith and trust, and a sprinkling of Tinker Bell's pixie dust. Then out of the nursery window they sailed, heading for Never Land, while Nana barked frantically from the ground below.

Back in Never Land, on his pirate ship, Captain Hook was grumbling about Peter Pan. You see, once in a fair fight, long ago, Peter had cut off one of the pirate captain's hands, so that he had to wear a hook in its place. Then Peter threw the hand to a crocodile, who had been lurking around ever since, hoping to nibble at the rest of Hook. Fortunately for the pirate, the crocodile had also swallowed a clock. He went *tick-tock, tick-tock* all day long, which gave a warning to Captain Hook.

Now, as Captain Hook grumbled about his young enemy, there was a call from the crow's nest, high up on the mast.

'Peter Pan, ahoy!'

'What? Where?' shouted Captain Hook, twirling his spyglass at the sky. And then he spied Peter and the children, pausing for a rest on a cloud. 'Swoggle me eyes, it is Pan!' Hook said gloatingly. 'Pipe up the crew ... Man the guns ...We'll get him this time at last!'

'Oh, Peter, it's just as I've dreamed it would be – the Mermaid Lagoon and all,' Wendy was saying when – suddenly – the first of the pirates' cannonballs ripped through the cloud close beneath their feet and went sizzling on past!

'Look out!' cried Peter. 'Tinker Bell, take Wendy and the boys to the island. I'll stay here and draw Hook's fire!'

Away flew Tinker Bell, as fast as she could go. In her naughty little heart she hoped the children would fall behind and be lost. She was especially jealous of Wendy who seemed to have won Peter Pan's heart.

Straight through the Never Land jungle Tink flew, down into a clearing beside an old dead tree called Hangman's Tree. She landed on a toadstool, bounced to a shiny leaf, and *pop!*, a secret door opened for her in the knot of the hollow tree.

*Zip!* Down a slippery tunnel Tink slid. She landed at the bottom in an underground room – the secret house of Peter Pan.

*Ting-a-ling!* she jingled, flitting from one corner of the room to the next. She was trying to awaken the sleeping Lost Boys.

At last, rather grumpily, they woke up and stretched in their little fur suits. And they listened to Tinker Bell.

'What? Peter Pan wants us to shoot down a terrible Wendy bird? Lead us to it!' they shouted, and out they hurried.

When Wendy and Michael and John appeared, flying wearily, the Lost Boys tried to pelt them with stones and sticks – especially the 'Wendy bird.' Down tumbled Wendy, all her happy thoughts destroyed – for without them no one can fly.

'Hurray! We got the Wendy bird!' the Lost Boys shouted.

But then Peter Pan arrived. How angry he was when he discovered that the boys had tried to shoot down Wendy, even though he had caught her before she could be hurt.

'I brought her to be a mother to us all and to tell us stories,' Peter said.

'All right, men,' he announced to the excited boys. 'Go and capture some Indians. Come on, Wendy, I'll show you the mermaids.'

So Peter and Wendy flew away, and the boys marched off through the forest, hopping over rocks and singing through the fields. There were wild animals all around, but the boys never thought to be afraid, until they spotted footprints.

'First we must surround them!' John cried, trying his very best to be a worthy leader. 'Then we'll take them by surpri –!'

*WHOOP!* The Never Land Indians ambushed the boys and carried them away to their camp.

The boys thought their capture was only a game – but the chief was furious. He thought they had kidnapped his daughter.

'Don't worry, the Indians are our friends,' the Lost Boys said, but the Indian Chief looked very stern.

Meanwhile, on the other side of the island, Wendy and Peter were visiting the mermaids in their peaceful Mermaid Lagoon. As they were chatting together, Peter suddenly said, 'Hush!'

A boat from the pirate ship was going by. In it was the wicked Captain Hook and Smee, the pirate cook. And at the stern, bound with ropes, sat Princess Tiger Lily, the Indian Chief's daughter.

'We'll make her talk,' Captain Hook said with a sneer. 'She'll tell us where Pan lives, or we'll leave her tied to slippery Skull Rock, where the tide will wash over her.'

But proud and loyal Tiger Lily would not say a single word.

Peter and Wendy flew to Skull Rock. Peter imitated Hook's voice, and tried to trick Smee into setting Tiger Lily free. That almost worked, but Hook discovered the trick, and came after Peter with his sword. Then, what a thrilling duel they had, all over that rocky cave where Princess Tiger Lily sat, with the tide up to her chin!

Peter won the duel and rescued Tiger Lily just in the nick of time. Away he flew to the Indian village, to see the princess safely home. And Wendy came along, too.

When Peter and Wendy brought Tiger Lily back, the Indian Chief set all the captives free. Then, what a wonderful feast they had! All the boys did Indian dances and learned wild Indian chants, and Peter Pan was made a chief!

While they all enjoyed the celebration, Smee crept up through the undergrowth and captured Tinker Bell.

Trapped in his cap, she struggled and kicked, but Smee took her back to the pirate ship and presented her to Captain Hook.

'Ah, Miss Bell,' said Hook, pretending to be kind. 'I've heard how badly Peter Pan has treated you since that scheming girl, Wendy, came along. How nice it would be if we could kidnap her and take her off to sea to scrub the decks and cook for the pirate crew!'

Tink jingled happily at the thought.

'But, alas,' said Hook with a sigh, 'we don't know where Pan's house is, so we cannot get rid of Wendy for you.'

Tink thought this over. 'You won't hurt Peter?' she asked, in solemn jingling tones.

'Of course not!' said Hook.

Then Tink marched to a map of Never Land and traced a path to Peter's hidden house.

'Thank you, my dear,' said the wicked Captain Hook, and he locked her up in a lantern cage, while he set off to capture Peter Pan!

That night when Wendy tucked the children into their beds in the underground house, she talked to them about home and their mother and father. Soon they were all so homesick that they wanted to leave at once. Wendy invited all the Lost Boys to come and live with the Darling family. Only Peter refused to go. He simply looked the other way as Wendy and the boys told him goodbye and climbed the tunnel to Hangman's Tree.

Up in the woods near Hangman's Tree, Hook and his pirate band were lying in wait. As each boy came out, a hand was clapped over his mouth and he was quickly tied up with ropes. Last of all came Wendy. *Zip, zip*, she was bound up, too, and the crew marched off with their load of children, back to the pirate ship.

'Blast it!' muttered Hook. 'We still don't have Pan!'

So he and Smee left a wicked bomb, wrapped as a gift from Wendy, for poor Peter to find. Very soon, they hoped, Peter would open it and blow himself straight out of Never Land.

Imagine how terrible Tinker Bell felt when she saw that all the children had been taken prisoner. She knew it was her fault!

The children were given the terrible choice between becoming pirates or walking the plank. To the boys, the life of a pirate sounded fine, sad to say, and they were all ready to join up. But Wendy was shocked. 'Never!' she cried.

'Very well,' said Hook. 'Then you shall be the first to walk the plank, my dear.'

Everyone felt so awful – though Wendy was ever so brave – that no one noticed when Tinker Bell escaped and flew off to warn Peter Pan.

What a dreadful moment it was when Wendy said good-bye and bravely walked out onto the long narrow plank.

And then she disappeared. Everyone listened, breathless, waiting for a splash, but not a single sound came! What could the silence mean?

Then they heard a familiar, happy cry. It was Peter Pan in the rigging, high above. Warned by Tinker Bell, he had arrived just in time to scoop up Wendy as she fell and fly with her to safety.

'This time you have gone too far, Hook!' Peter shouted.

He swooped down from the rigging, all set for a duel. And what a duel it was!

While they fought, Tinker Bell slashed the ropes that bound the boys, and they stopped the pirates from jumping overboard and rowing away in their boat. Then Peter knocked Hook's sword overboard, and Hook jumped, too. When the children last saw the evil Captain Hook, he was swimming for the boat, with the crocodile *tick-tocking* hungrily behind him.

Peter Pan took command of the pirate ship. 'Heave those halyards. Up with the jib. We're sailing to London!' he cried.

'Oh, Michael! John!' shouted Wendy. 'We're going home!'

And sure enough, with happy thoughts and faith and trust, and a liberal sprinkling of pixie dust, away flew the pirate ship. It sailed through the skies till the gangplank reached the Darlings' nursery windowsill.

But now that they arrived, the Lost Boys did not want to stay. 'We've decided to stay with Peter,' they said.

So Wendy, John and Michael waved goodbye as Peter Pan's ship took off into the sky, carrying the Lost Boys home to Never Land, where they still live today.

*Walt Disney's Peter Pan* is a *Disney Storybook Favourites* book

*Walt Disney's Peter Pan,* copyright © 1952, 2001, 2004 Disney Enterprises, Inc.
Story adapted by Monique Peterson. Illustrations adapted by John Hench and Al Dempster.

This edition was adapted and published in 2009 by
The Reader's Digest Association Limited
11 Westferry Circus, Canary Wharf, London E14 4HE

Editor: Rachel Warren Chadd
Designer: Louise Turpin
Design consultant: Simon Webb

® Reader's Digest, the Pegasus logo and Reader's Digest Young Families
are registered trademarks of
The Reader's Digest Association, Inc.

We are committed both to the quality of our products
and the service we provide to our customers.
We value your comments, so please do contact us on
08705 113366 or via our website at
www.readersdigest.co.uk
If you have any comments or suggestions
about the content of our books, email us at
gbeditorial@readersdigest.co.uk

Printed in China

A Disney Enterprises/Reader's Digest Young Families Book

ISBN 978 0 276 44454 8
Book code 641-013 UP0000-1
Oracle code 504400001H.00.24